CIPHERS
OF THE
SEA

ISHAN SRIJIT

INDIA · SINGAPORE · MALAYSIA

ISBN
Paperback 979-8-89699-449-7
Hardcase 979-8-89777-308-4

CHAPTER 1

"BZZZ! BZZZ! BZZZ!"

The alarm clock went off. Little disjointed green lines made the figure of '06:00 AM' on the wide display.

"I can't believe it's morning already!" I pulled the edge of the duvet over my half-open eyes. I wanted to sleep a little more but remembered that the ship would leave the dock at 10 am.

My friends and I were going to Morocco.

It was already 6:15 am. The problem with watching short video reels is there are no absolute boundaries of time or subject.

I should have slept early.

I better get going.

I dragged myself out of bed and went to the baño to get ready. That's what they call the bathroom. In the last 2 months, I have been in Spain, I have picked up only a few words and phrases. I could have done better. 'Learn Spoken Spanish in 30 days' was neatly tucked in the bookshelf gathering dust.

I quickly made a pineapple jam sandwich for breakfast and packed two more for the road. Just then I heard a car honk. I stretched my neck to look outside the window. Taxis with the typical bright yellow stripes were parked outside. My friends had arrived. We were all a part of the International Youth Exchange Language Immersion Program at the prestigious Instituto de Lenguas y Culturas at Cádiz. We were traveling as part of an arts program, to study Morocco's music, art, and historical landmarks.

I could still hear the loud music through the closed window panes. I'm sure the driver isn't amused. What did he expect from 14-15-year-olds? He has been there.

We were all excited about this group tour. There is so much to do in Marrakech. It should be a low of 10°C and high of 20°C, not very different from Cádiz.

I swiftly grabbed my bag and rushed out, making sure the door closed behind me. Carlos was standing outside the car, smiling.

Carlos Jiminez was originally from Spain and knew more about the city than most tour guides. He always ran his fingers over his short, wavy black hair, which suited his dark brown eyes and tanned skin. He hated early mornings. This was an exception.

"Alex! Carrying your Gameboy as always?" He shouted, looking at my backpack, grinning.

"You bet!", I replied. He was right. Three things describe me: video games, building gadgets, and comic books.

"Get in, guys!", shouted Yuki, from inside the taxi. Yuki Tanaka was Japanese, an armchair historian, and an aspiring manga artist who enjoyed telling stories. She had long, straight black hair, fair skin, and delicate features. She carried an artistic aura about her.

I looked inside both cars, but couldn't see Aisha. "Where's Aisha?" I asked.

"We will pick her up on the way," Liam said. He was riding shotgun. I waved to the rest of the gang and got into the taxi. The music was indeed loud.

We shortly reached Aisha's house. We honked and waited. After waiting a few minutes, when Aisha didn't step out, Liam walked over to her house and rang the doorbell.

We could see the door cracking open, but not fully. We saw Liam talking animatedly, and he finally turned back to look at us and shrugged. Sensing something was wrong, Yuki quickly got out, and Fatima, too, joined from the other taxi. They both walked up to Aisha's door and, after a minute of talking at the door, went inside.

Liam came back to update us. He spoke gravely, "She doesn't want to go on the trip. She says that the ship will crash and we'll all die." He had a worried look. He suddenly burst out laughing. As if on cue, Carlos and I joined him. Liam was the carefree kind. He was passionate about one thing – soccer, and he wanted to be a professional player. His tall and athletic build with short, messy, sandy blonde hair and blue eyes made heads turn. Liam O'Connor preferred living for the moment.

After about ten minutes, and multiple glances at our watches, what seemed like an eternity, the three girls walked out. Yuki walked in the front and gestured with a quick blink of her eyes to indicate that things were under control. She carried Aisha's bag.

Aisha Patel was from India and liked wearing her long black hair in a braid. Her warm brown skin and bright brown eyes perfectly complemented her fit build. She was a naturalist with a keen interest in environmental science.

Aisha chose to sit with Yuki in our taxi, and Carlos took the other taxi. Aisha was still disturbed. "I have a feeling the Mistral is going to crash, and we all will die!" She cried.

"You should manifest good thoughts, Aisha. We are what we think," replied Yuki. Yuki believed in the power of manifestation. Aisha finally agreed, though reluctantly.

"That's right, Aisha!" said Liam, still looking ahead at the road. "Manifestation will soon become a religion." There was a hint of sarcasm in his voice.

"Manifestation totally works, Liam!" Yuki spoke firmly. "If you really want something and imagine it as it was truly happening, the universe listens and makes it happen."

"So, if I just dream about scoring a goal in my next game, you are saying I can make it happen. Eh?"

"That's where you are wrong. Manifestation isn't just dreaming. It's your dream and action. Athletes use visualization all the time. They imagine winning, and it helps them perform better. Manifestation works the same way. Your thoughts guide your actions."

"I guess if manifestation helps someone stay motivated, there's no harm. All I'm saying is we should also give credit to hard work."

"Of course! It's the power of belief combined with hard work. No one should depend solely on manifestation."

The taxi took the turn towards the Algericas dock.

We reached the dock a little after 7.30 am. Our eyes fell upon the magnificent 'Mistral', towering over the dock with its gleaming white hull, in all its pride and glory.

Fatima passed along some 'Rooh Afza' in small pet bottles. It was a concentrated syrup made from a mix of herbal extracts, flowers, and fruits. Fatima loved cooking and experimenting with food. She was our go-to person whenever we needed some real food and not the refrigerated packaged food we usually bought at the store. She had mixed the syrup with cold milk and was a perfect, refreshing, start to the day. Fatima Al-Mansoori was from Morocco and was excited about meeting her family. Her dark curly hair often fell over her face, touching her olive skin and expressive brown eyes.

Mohammed Idris hung up his call and joined us. He was on his mobile phone telling his parents and sisters in Nigeria that he had reached the dock. 'Moe', as we called him, had short black hair, a medium brown complexion, and bright, curious eyes. He was athletic and slightly taller than average. He was passionate about soccer and when he and Liam met all we heard were terms such as 'Nutmeg', Clean Sheet', 'Volley', and 'Counter Attack'.

We waited for the announcement.

Chapter 2

Awoman with a distinct Spanish accent sounded over the speakers: "All passengers of Mistral proceed to Counter Number 3. Thank you."

We all rushed to the counter where a tall woman with blonde hair, wearing an elegant blue uniform, checked our papers, consent forms, and tickets and stamped our passports. Our luggage was tagged and taken to the ship separately.

After the standard security check and baggage screening, we went through a long gangway and boarded the ship. After boarding, we all assembled in a designated area, where the Cruise Director, a large, burly man of about 40, conducted a safety briefing, which included emergency procedures, the location of life jackets, and lifeboat stations. We were also given a crash course on what to do in case of an emergency.

My eyes, however, were fixated on the magnificent mosaic of a hammer shark on the wall of the ship.

The ship set sail at 10 am as scheduled.

We all went to our cabins on the main deck. Each cabin had 4 bunk beds. Liam, Carlos, Moe, and I shared one cabin. The adjacent cabin was occupied by Yuki, Aisha, and Fatima. The cabin had a bathroom with shower, TV, air conditioning, a chair and a table fixed to the floor, and a storage area. A painting of a clownfish adorned the wall and brought some life to the otherwise staid room. It was noon already and we decided to have our lunch. The meal timings were given to us in advance. Breakfast (7:00 AM - 9:00 AM), Lunch (12:00 PM - 2:00 PM), Dinner (6:00 PM - 8:00 PM). There were multiple dining options, including a buffet with Mediterranean cuisine, snacks, and beverages.

After lunch, we set out to explore the ship. Mistral was about 230 meters in length, with 12 decks in total, out of which 10 were passenger decks. More than 600 crew managed the ship, which had a passenger capacity of more than 1300. The Passenger Deck had well-designed cabins, accommodating 2-4 people per cabin. Each cabin had amenities like a bathroom, air conditioning, and storage space. There was a large cafeteria-style restaurant serving meals with both buffet and à la carte options. There was also a lounge area with comfortable seating and tables, offering games, books, and a small library. The Upper Deck was an open Observation Deck with lounge chairs and shaded spots for relaxation while enjoying the views. It was perfect for watching the sunset or spotting marine life. They also had an entertainment lounge with a small stage for live music, movie screenings, and activities like trivia nights. The Sun Deck had a small swimming pool for cooling off, surrounded by sun loungers. There was also a designated area for kids with games and activities.

We spent the day playing card games, talking about Morocco, and enjoying the beautiful sunset. The darkness set in fast. The temperature dipped. The stars seemed unusually bright in the clear sky.

Liam, Moe, and I went back to our cabin. Carlos wanted to stay back and enjoy the solitude. I hit the bed. I slept thinking about where we must be in the Strait of Gibraltar.

Chapter 3

"BZZZ! BZZZ! BZZZ!"

The buzzer in my watch went off. Last night, I slept like a rock. And for good reason. I slept early. There was no Internet. No reels. No mindless scrolling.

I swiftly got out of bed. Liam was already up, going through some brochures of the ship. Moe and Carlos were not there. Just then both of them barged into the room looking flustered.

"Aisha is at it again", Carlos threw his hands up in the air. "She says we are going to crash!"

"It's started playing on my mind too." Moe sounded frustrated. Liam sneered.

Aisha did not join us for breakfast. I was getting worried. We all decided to go and talk to her. As we entered her cabin, we saw Aisha sitting on the bed, holding her head. She raised her head to look at us. "We are going to die. We all will die. I told you we shouldn't do this trip." She muttered and started crying.

I sat by her side. "Why are you talking like this, Aisha? This is just a 3-day trip. We will be in Marrakech the day after." I said.

Aisha looked at me with surprise. "Don't you understand? We are going in the wrong direction. There is something wrong with the navigation. We are going to die." She couldn't stop her tears.

Fatima sat on her other side, gave her a side hug and said, "Ok, Aisha. We will check with the captain. I'm sure if there is something wrong, he will find a solution."

Aisha's eyes lit up. She looked at Fatima. "Will you do that? Thank you! Ask him to turn back while we still can." She said. Fatima nodded. While Carlos and Yuki stayed back with Aisha, we all went to see the captain.

We knew Aisha as someone with a heightened state of intuition. She usually knew things before they happened. I shrugged off the thought. This was different. We were in expert hands. There has not been a single reported incident of navigation errors on these cruises. At least not that we know of.

The captain was unavailable, so we met the First Officer. Alejandro was a 30-something man with an athletic build and full of energy. He was also Carlos' distant cousin. We did not know how to broach the topic.

Moe spoke hesitantly. "Sir, we are glad to be a part of this cruise. We are excited about going to Morocco.

But … one of our friends is worried that we are maybe sailing in the wrong direction." We suddenly realized how silly that sounded. However, Alejandro listened intently. With the air of someone who hears such fears every day, he replied, "Sure. We will check the navigation and the course again. I will speak to the captain." When we turned to walk away, he said, "The captain has been sailing for 30 years. You are in safe hands." He smiled and walked away. We stood there, smiling bashfully.

Over the day, we forgot about the conversation. We spent our time playing cards and planning the sights to see in Marrakech. Aisha now seemed at ease as the First Officer himself had assured everything is in control.

Towards evening, the weather changed. It had started raining. We stayed in the cabin playing the board games Fatima had brought.

'Knock. Knock.' There was someone at the door. Liam opened the door. Alejandro stood with a troubled look, visibly shaken.

CHAPTER 4

Alejandro spoke nervously.

The captain had misread a crucial navigational chart due to sudden weather changes and a malfunctioning GPS system. However, confident despite the conditions, the captain had decided to press on without rerouting. Now, we were off course and the weather was changing.

"But there's nothing to worry. We are using radar systems and Automatic Identification Systems to detect other vessels and obstacles. We are also trying to communicate with other ships nearby to confirm positions. This is standard procedure. Don't worry. We are getting you to land safely." Alejandro said, his words coming out in a rush. His expression betrayed his words.

We were shocked.

Alejandro quickly turned around and ran back. The door closed itself.

Aisha clutched her pillow and pulled into a corner of the bed. There was fear in her eyes. We all looked at each other. Nobody had planned for this.

"We should pack our bags," Moe spoke in a frantic tone.

We packed our bags, put essentials in our backpacks and waited for the weather to clear. Our ears were strained to the intercom, waiting to hear that we were on course and safe.

"Should I go and check with Alejandro?" asked Liam.

Suddenly we heard a deep, resonant blast of a horn. It was low-pitched and steady, followed by silence.

"It is the foghorn!" Exclaimed Yuki. "They are trying to alert other ships."

We waited impatiently, praying for this moment to pass.

After a few minutes, the intercom buzzed.

"Attention, passengers. This is Captain Hans Richter speaking. We are currently experiencing some unexpected, severe weather conditions. There is no need to panic. I want to assure you that our crew is well-trained and fully prepared to handle the situation.

For your safety, I kindly ask everyone to please clear the open decks and return to your cabins immediately. Stay calm and remain indoors until we notify you that it is safe to come out.

We appreciate your cooperation and understanding. Thank you for your attention, and we will keep you updated as we navigate through this weather."

His voice was steady and authoritative, yet there was an underlying tension that we couldn't ignore.

Several minutes passed. We looked out through the porthole – the small oval window in the cabin. All we could see was darkness.

The ship kept sounding the foghorn.

Suddenly, without warning, the ship swayed left to right like a giant swing. We lost our balance and fell. We held onto fixtures in the cabin, trying to gain our balance.

There was a sudden loud, piercing siren changing in pitch and intensity. It alternated between high and low, with an oscillating effect.

Just then, the ship swayed a little more, and Yuki spoke, shaking, "What if we capsize as Aisha said?" Her voice shook. I tried checking my phone. No network.

The intercom buzzed again.

"Attention, passengers. This is Captain Hans Richter. We are currently navigating through a significant storm. For your safety, I urge everyone to remain in your cabins if you haven't already done so.

Our crew is working diligently to steer the ship out of this storm, and I assure you that we are well-prepared for this situation. Please stay calm, avoid the open decks, and keep your safety gear nearby.

We will keep you updated as we progress. Thank you for your cooperation and understanding."

There was a notable urgency in the way he spoke this time.

"Why is he asking us to keep our safety gear ready?", Fatima asked.

CHAPTER 5

The ship suddenly did what appeared to be a nosedive and then went up almost instantly. We were thrown off our balance again. We were flung across the cabin. I hit my arm on the bunk bed. I could hear screams. Moe and Fatima, maybe. But it was difficult to tell. Things, carefully arranged on the table, found their place on the floor, rolling about. The door of the cabin was flung open.

We could hear the wind howling like a wild animal. The sound pierced through the steel walls of the ship. I could only see darkness through the porthole. The ship lurched violently, tossing us around as if we were rag dolls. In the commotion, I saw that Liam was bleeding from his forehead. I turned to look at others. Fatima and Aisha were clutching onto the bunk bed. I couldn't see Carlos. Yuki seemed in pain, huddled in one corner holding onto the table. Just then the ship swayed and I slid towards the washroom. I vainly flapped my arms trying to find imaginary objects to hold on to, and hit my back to the bathroom door. Pain shot through my spine.

Outside, people were shouting and speaking loudly. Screams of pain and agony. But as if in a competition to be the loudest boy in the class, the roar of the wind drowned out all other sounds. It was a deafening symphony of chaos.

Carlos shouted from somewhere behind me, "This is just a bad storm. Maybe it will pass." We all knew he didn't believe in it.

Moe shouted, "Everyone, listen! We need to stay together. Don't panic!" His voice, usually confident, trembled slightly.

Liam said forcing a strained smile, "This is awesome! We'll have a story to tell!" His bravado was a mask for his fear. He was clutching the bunk railing, fear in his eyes.

Fatima yelled, "Please, let's stay together. If we get separated, we won't make it!"

The siren seemed to be getting louder.

The intercom buzzed again.

"Attention, passengers. This is your captain. We are facing an emergency, and I must ask everyone to prepare to abandon ship immediately!

Please proceed to your nearest lifeboat station and follow the instructions of our crew. Do not rush or push; your safety is our priority.

Remember to wear your life jacket, take only essential items, and leave all luggage behind.

Stay together, stay calm, and we will get through this safely.

We will ensure everyone is accounted for once we reach the lifeboats. Thank you for your cooperation."

His voice was shaky.

This is it. This is serious.

The storm intensified. The waves rattled the metal of the ship, making it creak and groan as it fought against the onslaught. The sound of violent waves relentlessly crashed against the hull. The lights flickered and dimmed.

"Let's go! Grab only essentials!" Fatima shouted.

"*All passengers to lifeboats…*" the voice on the speaker crackled and died.

We picked our shoulder bags with essentials. We staggered forward unsteadily to the nearest lifeboat station, bracing ourselves against the walls, gripping the railings, as the ship rocked wildly from side to side. There was chaos everywhere.

On the deck, crewmen were lining up the passengers to board the lifeboats.

I looked around and saw how menacing and ferocious the sea looked. Towering waves crashed against the ship, spraying water over us. It was dark all around as if we were in the middle of black.

Suddenly, the storm peaked, and another colossal wave crashed against the ship, throwing it off balance.

I could hear the sound of the hull cracking under the pressure. Panic erupted as passengers screamed and rushed to the lifeboats, breaking the lines, some losing balance and rolling on the floor. People were screaming and crying. We held the railings firmly and staggered across the deck, trying to keep our footing as the ship pitched and rolled, determined to survive. We were amongst the last to reach the lifeboat station.

The ship tilted dangerously, and we grabbed onto each other. The storm seemed to be testing our bond. Finally, the ship began to break apart. We made a desperate leap into the lifeboat as we watched in horror the mighty Mistral, slowly swallowed by the sea. There were still some crew on deck.

All of us had managed to board the lifeboat. Some of us had lost our bags. But we were together. The storm raged on, but we clung to each other. We saw other lifeboats in the distance, but we all seemed to be going in different directions, led by the storm. Cries were soon replaced with silence of fear. Nobody spoke.

The storm eventually calmed. The rain stopped. I couldn't see anything. It was dark everywhere.

After several hours, the lifeboat kept bobbing. We didn't move. It was cold, wet, and scary. We didn't know where we were, how far from land, and if other ships were coming for rescue.

The sky slowly changed color. The daylight was breaking. In the dim light, we looked around.

We seemed to have reached land! It seems that for several hours we have been near land! The current had carried us to the shore. We will finally be home!

Liam jumped into the water, holding the rope of the boat and pulled us towards the land. I joined in.

The ordeal was over.

Chapter 6

We slowly climbed out of the boat, the cool water lapping around our ankles. We waded through the gentle waves, laughing through our parched lips. We walked through the golden sand and crashed on the beach. Liam and Carlos tied the boat securely to a large rock, ensuring it wouldn't drift away with the tide.

We were lucky to be alive. I looked around for other boats but couldn't find any. We all looked wasted, but at least we were together. I had hurt my back. With each movement, it pained. I saw that Liam had a big bump on his forehead. Moe had hit his left elbow somewhere, and it was swollen. Yuki had maybe twisted her ankle because she couldn't even stand due to the pain. Aisha had a broken nose. Apart from these minor injuries, we were fine.

The beach was pristine. Thankfully the authorities are doing a good job of keeping it clean. There were coconut trees everywhere and nice thick vegetation. Perfect spot for a summer getaway.

We walked to the beach, kept our bags down and looked around to spot a tourist, fishing folks, or any locals. We had to call home, school, friends. They would have heard about the storm and would be worried.

"It's likely that nobody knows about the storm. The communication lines were broken," said Aisha. "We should reach out to the authorities immediately. They could carry out rescue missions. Several boats were headed in the wrong direction." She added with deep concern.

Not seeing anyone, Carlos finally looked towards the island and shouted, "Hello! Helloooo! Oyeee!" We expected to see some movement, a speedboat, lifeguards, and tourists about to walk in carrying their mats, surprised to see their spot already taken. But there were none. Maybe, it is too early in the day.

Was this a private property?

Fatima and Aisha volunteered to go further inside and check for people or roads. Moe and Carlos went along. Liam wanted to lie on the beach for some more time, soaking in the experience. He laughed and said, "What an experience. But you bet I don't want to be doing it again."

Yuki was unable to walk so she stayed back. I looked around my backpack to find a heat spray and sat down to examine Yuki's ankle. She reached out for a crepe bandage.

All four returned in about 30 minutes. We looked at them with anticipation.

"Well?" I asked. The look in their eyes was worrying.

Aisha spoke in a shaky voice, each word laced with fear, "This is a small island and looks uninhabited. There are only trees and sand everywhere. Lots of coconut and banana trees."

Moe added, "And there are caves, so you could be sure there are wild animals."

"We are in the middle of nowhere, guys!" Carlos said in a rushed, breathless manner.

Our hearts sank. It took some time for us to accept the reality.

Finally, Liam asked, "So, what do we do now?"

"We wait and stay alive till we are found. I'm sure the rescue teams have already started their search," Fatima said, with a flicker of determination and hope.

Once we had come to terms with the reality, our next step was to ensure our survival till we were found.

Yuki said, "We need to find a stream or a freshwater source. Water is the most important resource for us."

We split into two teams, scouring the island. Aisha, Carlos, and I made one team. Liam and Fatima took the west. Moe stayed back with Yuki.

We trekked through dense foliage, climbing over roots and pushing aside branches. There were large trees, oak, cypress, and shrubs. After some time, we stumbled upon a small, clear stream. The water was the clearest I had ever seen. We filled our bottles and cupped our hands to drink.

"This is amazing!" Aisha exclaimed, splashing water on Carlos, who laughed but quickly shushed her. There was rustling in the bushes nearby. We froze.

Something slithered in the bushes.

The jungle appeared denser. It could be wild animals. After a few minutes, Carlos broke the silence, "We have to find a way out. We don't know what's on this island. Poisonous snakes, monkeys, scorpions, poisonous berries. There's no food, no bed, no shelter."

"We are not here by choice, Carlos," Aisha said. Our frustration was showing.

We walked back to the beach.

As the day passed, we felt more and more hungry. We plucked some bananas. These bananas were the most delicious ones I had ever had. Moe pointed to the coconut trees, full of coconuts. These would be good sources of natural electrolytes. I had seen coconut trees earlier but these were much taller and thinner than what I remembered. We found the ones which were shorter than the rest.

Moe found a bamboo pole, about 15 feet in length, and with the deftness of a skilled survival expert, he took another small stick, and using a flexible vine, which he found nearby, tied them together to make a 'V' shape. We watched in amazement as he made a 'fruit picker'. Moe was a boy scout. He knew what he was doing.

Liam saw all the attention Moe was getting and volunteered to be the one to pluck the coconuts. Moe and I offered to help, but Liam wanted the limelight. Standing under the tree, he stretched his arms upwards, holding the pole. But it was one thing holding it parallel to the ground and another thing balancing it vertically straight. He kept swaying on all sides trying to balance the pole. We all started laughing at the sight. This angered Liam and he tried even harder to hold the bamboo straight. The more he tried, the more he reminded us of equilibrists in circuses. He kept moving away from the coconut tree doing his balancing act. He didn't even know where he was going. He stepped on a coconut frond, slipped and fell on all fours. We all burst out laughing. "Once more! Once more! Once more!" We all chanted. Liam looked at us and started laughing himself.

Carlos and I joined Liam in holding the pole, keeping it straight and resting its top on the trunk of the coconut tree. We slowly pushed it upwards to reach the bunch of coconuts. Once the 'V' shape was hooked to a bunch, we pulled with all our strength. A huge bunch of coconuts fell. We scattered on all sides to avoid the rain of coconuts.

We gathered the coconuts and kept them together.

Moe attempted to crack open the coconut, by hitting it against rocks. With each swing against the rocks, Moe felt the resistance of the tough shell, and what he thought would be a simple task turned out to be much harder than he anticipated. With repeated strikes, the husk started giving away, but it remained stubbornly intact. Frustrated, we finally decided to give up.

The day was getting dark and the temperature started dropping. We didn't have a place to sleep. "Let's use bamboo shafts and banana leaves to make a shelter," Aisha said.

"Good idea," said Moe. "Let's also use the dried coconut fronds. These will serve as good protection from the weather."

"Let's put it up right here on the beach, as it's closer to water and away from any possible wildlife," said Liam.

But Carlos was not comfortable. "Let's go further inside. If the water levels rise, we will be in trouble."

"Let's not keep it very close to the sea, but not too much inside either. We have to be away from water and wild animals. Also, we should make some fire. It will help us be spotted by a ship or rescue team. Also, Yuki cannot walk very far." Fatima said. We all agreed.

Under Moe's supervision, we built a small shelter enough to house the seven of us. Moe had some waterproof box matches in his bag. We wondered how he managed to carry it. We gathered some dry twigs and leaves and made the fire. It was a warm, cozy, evening. We slept on a bed made of banana leaves and coconut fronds. We kept sticks close by in case snakes or other wild animals decided to visit us. Slowly, we slipped into sleep after a tiring day, our ears still straining to hear the sound of a boat, the siren of a ship, or the whirring of choppers.

Chapter 7

When I woke up, I saw Fatima and Liam, in the water holding crude bamboo spears, like javelin throwers. They walked till they could hold their balance in the gentle waves, their eyes fixed on the water, looking for fish.

I looked at the calm sea, which till a day back was, a chaotic expanse of towering waves rattling and tearing apart hard metal. I shook away that memory. I looked at the sky to see any signs of rescue missions. There were none.

Fatima and Liam were still holding their javelins.

"Let's try the stream", I said walking up to them, slowly dragging myself in the water, digging my heels into the sand, one step at a time. "I had spotted a few in shallow waters."

"That's a great idea!" Fatima said.

Fishing was tougher than we imagined. It's as if the fish knew. They dodged each stab of the pole.

After a grueling hour and some, Liam said, "This is not working. Maybe spear fishing isn't our thing. Let's try making a fish trap."

We spent a few minutes observing the direction in which the fish were swimming. Then we built a barrier using rocks, so that the fish were forced to swim into a small area from where it would be easy to catch them.

We finally had caught enough fish for a feast. We took them back to the beach.

We were missing the city, our friends, our classes, our teachers, the local deli, and even the oily steak. What would I give to be back in my bed? Once I'm back I will sleep in late. I will watch movies. I will spend the day at the park, watching people, knowing that home is near and I can go anytime.

Moe and Aisha neatly arranged some bamboo sticks to make a large sign on the beach. It read HELP.

Hopefully, some aircraft will see this. We had seen it in the movies.

The day passed by uneventfully. Bananas, some wild berries, fish, and then sitting together looking at the sea and sky.

As evening came, we lit the fire and sat around it. We spoke about our lives back home. Yuki started sobbing. Fatima too covered her head between her folded knees and started weeping. Aisha got up from her place near Liam and sat between Fatima and Yuki, holding them in a tight embrace. Under the smiling faces and brave exterior, we were scared and losing hope.

That night, no one spoke. We all lay down thinking of our families and friends. Chances of rescue was getting slimmer.

Chapter 8

"Let's explore the island. Sitting around here waiting for rescue is foolish." Yuki's frustration was clear in her words. "Maybe ships pass from the other side of the island," she added.

We had been looking towards the sky and sea since the day broke. We desperately needed a glimmer of hope – a distant ship, a rescue aircraft – but there was nothing. It seemed the waves too, were repeating the same dance routine. The clouds would frequently change its shape but they also seem to have run out of ideas.

We agreed that we should find out more about the island. Maybe we will get ideas to get out of this place.

"I can't shake the fear that we might stumble upon some forest dwellers on this island. I have heard some eerie stories, enough to send chills down my spine!" Carlos spoke. He had a fearful tone.

We set out on our expedition. Yuki's ankle was getting better. The swelling had subsided considerably, but it was still paining; she stayed back alone. However, she insisted that we go on without her.

The island was larger than we expected. We saw several species of colorful spiders along the way. There were many small and large caves. Some were so small that only small cats could enter, but some were big enough to house a pickup truck.

As we passed one of the caves, Aisha noticed a glimmering object stuck between two rocks. It was fluttering in the wind. We went closer. Moe pulled out the object. It was a tattered piece of silk cloth. The golden embroidery on the cloth reflected the sunlight. "It's just a piece of an old cloth," laughed Moe, and threw it away, starting to walk back.

"And how exactly did it get there?" Aisha asked. "It's not ours. So, either there are other people on this island, or someone has been here before us," she said.

I added, "That means, if they have managed to find their way out of this island, maybe we can too!"

"Yes!" Moe exclaimed.

Finally, there was hope. We all smiled.

"Unless we find their remains," Carlos said with a blank look. There was an uncomfortable moment of silence.

"C'mon Carlos! We will know only if we explore more. Let's not jump to conclusions. As Yuki says, we manifest what we say. Let's check the cave." Aisha said.

We shone our flashlights inside the cave. We had four flashlights between us. We saw that the cave inside was larger than what the entrance led us to believe. We carefully stepped inside, following Liam. There could be bats inside. Or worse, wild animals. We gripped our hiking sticks firmly as if preparing for an assault from a wild animal about to jump at us.

The roof of the cave was low, about 5 feet in height from the ground. We looked around but found nothing out of place. There were some rock pieces on the ground. Dried leaves had been swept inside the cave by the wind. After looking around for a while, disappointed, we decided to head out. The lack of oxygen in such a confined space was evident.

While we were heading out, in the darkness, Fatima bumped her toe on a rock and lost her balance. She lunged forward, frantically grasping Moe's shoulder to hold her balance. With her other hand, she held onto the wall of the cave. A rock dislodged from the wall and fell with a loud thud.

"Fatima, are you ok?" shouted Liam. We shone our flashlights to check on her. Liam shone his flashlight on the wall. There was a small gap from where the rock had fallen. There was something lodged in there. Liam took a closer look. It looked like paper. He pulled it out slowly.

It was a parchment, weathered over the years! It was rolled up neatly and pushed into the gap in the wall.

We crowded around to look at this newfound object. Moe took the parchment in his hands holding it carefully. "It's not paper. It's heavier." He was vibrating with enthusiasm. "And feels rougher than paper," said Fatima, taking her turn at holding it before handing it back to Liam. "Let's go outside and check this," Aisha said. The excitement was hard to contain.

After stepping out of the cave, Liam delicately kept the discovery on the ground and started to unwind it, careful not to damage it. The paper was unusually rough but sturdy. It felt almost like leather.

As Liam started to uncoil the parchment, our eyes fell upon the content. It was an intricate drawing of what looked like trees and cliffs. It was very meticulously drawn, with decorative ancient markings and symbols around the edges. Our hearts were racing. We looked at this piece of history with excitement as the unfurled scroll lay in front of us!

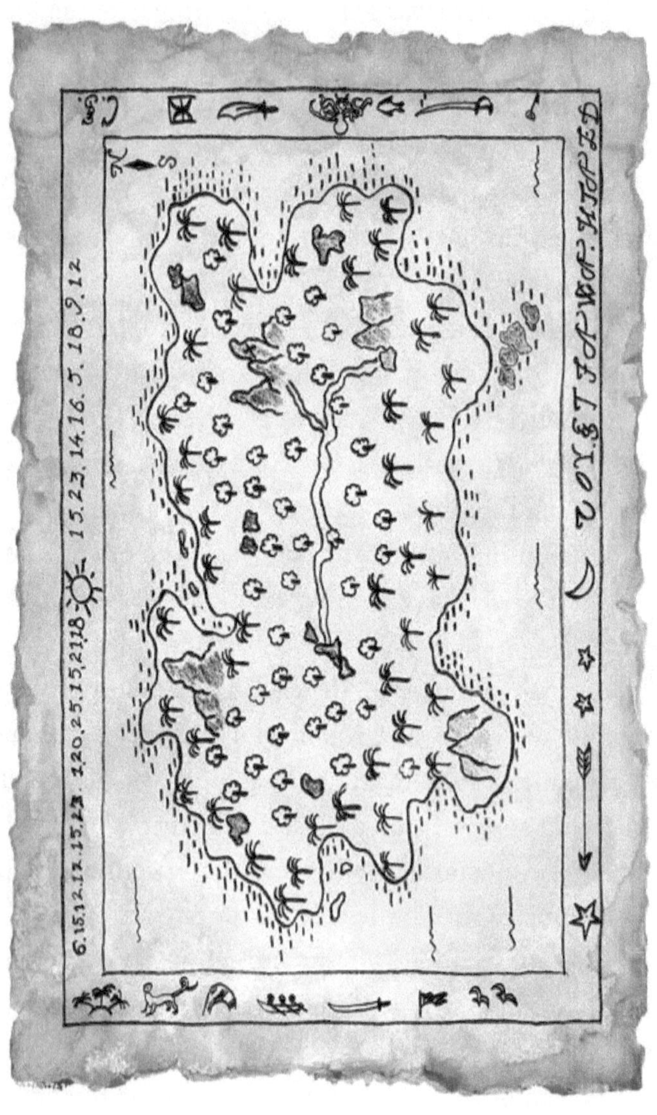

It was a parchment, weathered over the years!

It was a drawing, rectangular, about twenty-four by twelve inches, in size. It was illustrated with ornate drawings and strange images. It showed a large mass of land surrounded by water. The land mass showed rocky terrains, mountains, trees, and water bodies.

"This is the drawing of an island," Moe said.

"It could be this same island!" exclaimed Aisha.

"Maybe this was drawn by people who were marooned on this island before us, and they might have found an escape route! This could be a map showing us the way out of this island!" Carlos voiced our collective thoughts.

"True! Look here, there are compass directions on the top right. N and S, showing North and South," said Fatima excitedly.

"Ok. But where do we have to go?" Liam asked. "There are no directions!"

After a futile attempt at decoding the map, we decided to head back. We couldn't contain our excitement and wanted to share this discovery with Yuki. Then, we could sit together and figure out this map.

CHAPTER 9

Yuki looked at the map and stared at it with amazement. She spotted the letters written in one corner 'C.S.' Her eyes widened, fixed on the map. She looked at us with shock. "This is unbelievable!", she whispered, her voice trembling with awe.

"Guys, this has to be the drawn by Captain Salazar!", she cried, her hands trembling as she looked at the map.

We all looked at each other, not knowing what she meant.

We sat around her as Yuki shared the story of the famous pirate Captain Salazar, also known as *'Flat Nose'*, who ruled the Straits of Gibraltar.

Yuki had a natural interest in pirates and Vikings and had read about Captain Salazar. She told us the story of the dreaded pirate.

We listened intently as she spoke.

"In the heart of the Mediterranean, sailed a notorious pirate known as Captain Salazar. With a heart as fierce as a storm and a reputation that sent shivers down the spines of even the bravest sailors,

Salazar was a man both feared and admired. His ship, the *Savage Gale*, was said to be as swift as the wind, and its black sails would haunt the dreams of those who dared cross his path.

But Captain Salazar wasn't always the fearsome pirate, everyone knew him to be. He was born into a life of hardship in a small coastal village. His father, a humble fisherman, dreamed of a better life for his son. Young Salazar often gazed out at the ocean, listening to tales of adventure and treasure whispered by passing sailors. It wasn't long before the call of the sea grew too strong to resist.

As a young man, Salazar joined a crew of pirates, where he quickly proved his courage. He was cunning, resourceful, and fiercely loyal to his crewmates. But betrayal happens only with those who are close. One fateful night, after a successful raid on a merchant ship, a fierce storm blew in. In the chaos, Salazar's closest friend, a man known as Blackthorn, betrayed him, seeking the loot for himself. As lightning illuminated the dark sea, Blackthorn struck, stabbing the sleeping Salazar in the back, and throwing him overboard, leaving him to drown while Blackthorn escaped with the riches.

But fate had other plans. The sea saved Salazar. He emerged from the depths, not just a man but something more—a vengeful man fueled by betrayal. The ocean whispered to him, granting him dark powers and a new purpose: to protect the treasure he had once sought, a treasure that had been cursed by the blood of the betrayed.

From that day on, Captain Salazar roamed the seas, gathering a new crew of misfits, outcasts, and those wronged by fate. Together, they sought out the treasure: a chest filled with gold, jewels, and an ancient artefact said to hold the power of the sea itself.

Blackthorn was captured, tied to a rope, and dragged underneath the ship.

With each plunder, the curse grew stronger, making it clear that only the pure of heart could claim the treasure without facing dire consequences.

As the legend of Captain Salazar spread, tales of his cursed treasure became a warning for treasure hunters everywhere. Many sought to find it, but all who dared were met with storms, shipwrecks, and phantom of the vengeful captain himself, forever roaming the waters with a single purpose: to protect what was rightfully his.

Years passed, and the treasure remained hidden, buried deep in the sands of a mysterious island, watched over by the restless spirit of Captain Salazar. His story became folklore, a tale of betrayal and adventure, infused with the supernatural whispers of the sea. It was said that only those who understood the true value of friendship and loyalty would ever uncover the secret to the treasure—and perhaps even break the curse that bound Salazar's soul to the ocean."

We listened intently.

We were getting goosebumps. We realized that this scroll may be the key to uncovering something significant. Could this be the way to a secret treasure? Finally, there was something to look forward to on this island.

The night was falling and we decided to study the map in the morning.

That night was the longest. We all lay thinking about the map and the story of Captain Salazar. This was the same beach where dangerous pirates had once been. Their ships with big black flags would have anchored on this shore. Many of them might have spent their time on this exact spot where we lay right now listening to the sound of waves.

We were all awake. But none of us spoke. We were waiting for the day to break.

CHAPTER 10

We woke up excitedly the next day. None of us got much sleep. The story of Captain Salazar and his treasure kept ringing in our ears. We spent the night thinking of how he would have led his crew on Savage Gale, fought Blackthorn, and reclaimed his treasure.

When we looked, we saw Yuki hunched over the map, studying it carefully. "You guys are right. This could indeed be the island we are on," she shouted excitedly as soon as she saw us.

We walked towards where Yuki was sitting. Aisha said, "Ok! The question remains; while it gives the North and South compass directions, how do we use the map to reach the treasure?"

"More importantly, the question is where are WE on this map?" Liam added.

"From this beach, we don't see the sun rising, but we know it sets in front of us. So, we can be sure that we are facing the west," Yuki said, tilting her head sideways while reading the map.

"The top of the map is pointing to the north. If the north is up, the west will be on the left. This means we are on this side of the island, to the left of the map." I said, pointing to the left of the map.

"And this has to be a stream or a river," said Aisha, pointing to the wavy, narrow structure, a few inches to the right.

"But where are we going? This is the entire island. If at all this mythical pirate, Captain Salazar, has buried his treasure here, where are we headed to? It's not that he has left directions!" Liam sounded impatient.

"Look at this X mark here, right on this cliff. This is where we need to go. I'm sure that is where the treasure is. Else, he wouldn't mark it that way." Moe said, pointing to an X mark on one of the drawings, which looked like a range of mountains or hills.

"Correct! So, we cross the entire island from left to the right, to reach this place, which looks like a range of mountains," said Carlos.

"Great! Let's go get some treasure!" Moe was excited.

"Why are you so quiet, Aisha?" asked Yuki. "What are you thinking?"

Aisha was looking at the map intently, studying it, shaking her head.

"There is something wrong. Something is not quite right with this map." Aisha spoke.

She took a twig and drew on the sand.

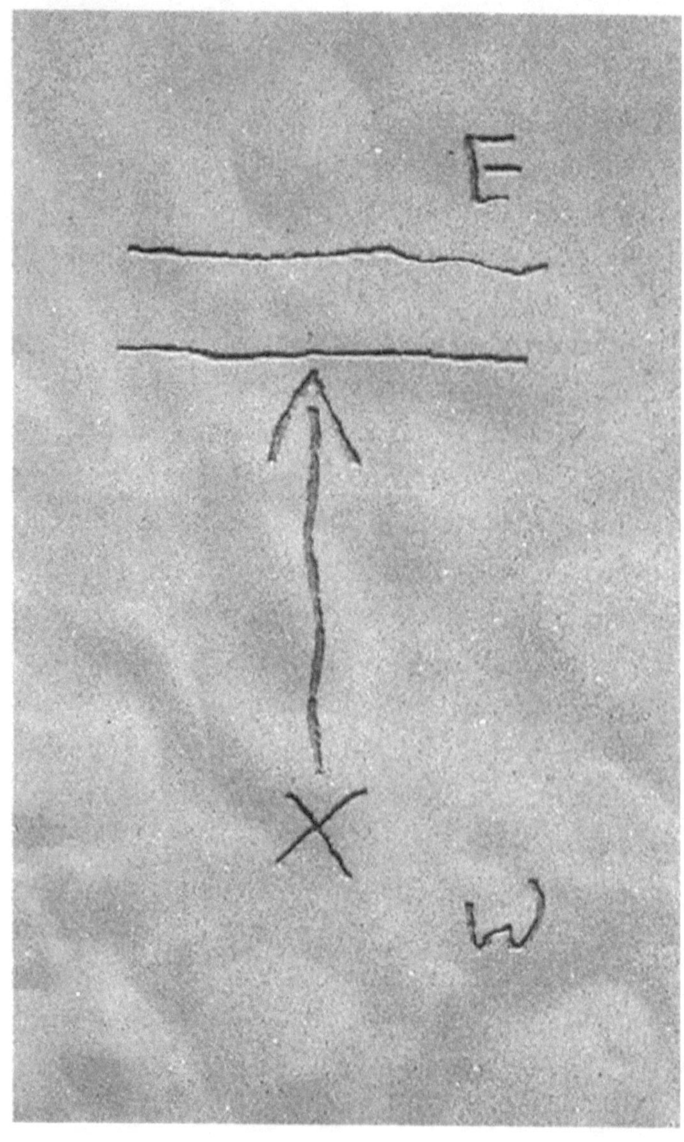

"This is our current location on this beach."

"This cross mark is our current location on this beach. We are on the West. When we trek up to the stream, we walk towards the East. And the stream flows through in front of us from left to right. But if we were to follow this map and hike towards the stream from the left of the map, as Alex said, we would end up reaching the stream's source!" Aisha exclaimed.

"True, and look at the coastline. It doesn't look like ours." Liam said.

"Guys! This is a map, and it was drawn at a time when there was no aerial photography or satellites. This map was, in all likelihood, drawn using their memory of walking through the island, exploring each location. There could be mistakes." Moe said impatiently.

"We also have to understand that the coastlines change over the years due to natural causes. They don't stay the same. Maybe this is what it looked like during those times." Carlos said.

"And it may not even be drawn to scale. It's just a crude illustration of the island." Moe added.

"What if this is not even the same island? Maybe the treasure, if at all there is one, is on some other island, which only Captain Salazar knew about?" Carlos said hesitantly.

We looked at each other. In our excitement, we had not thought about that possibility.

There was a brief moment of silence.

Aisha broke the silence. "They are not likely to leave the map of another island here. It doesn't make sense."

"Guys! Whatever it may be, what's the harm in following this map? Maybe, we will discover something. It's not like we have anything else to do!" Fatima said.

"Ok, it's settled then. We pack our backpacks and follow this trail. As per the map, this here is the North, so we are on the extreme left, which is west. We will walk and follow the stream to reach the cliff." Liam said.

We all agreed.

"No. Wait!" Yuki called out. She has been studying the map since Aisha raised her concern.

"This map is not what it seems. It was common for pirates to provide confusing directions in their maps. We know that the stream is in front of us when we walk into the island. If we forget for a moment about the compass directions on the map, we should be able to read the map differently. There are some remarkable clues on this map. Look, here, this drawing on top is a sun. Look at the bottom now. This is a moon, along with stars. This is not a random arrangement of pictures. I think this is to show that in reality, east is on top and west is at the bottom." Yuki elaborated.

"But doesn't the moon too rise in the east and set in the west?" Moe was confused.

"Yes, but maybe this is to show that it's night. Sun is Day and Moon is Night. They are generally considered opposites. Similarly, the sun being east, this moon here is west!" Aisha exclaimed eagerly.

The map now looked different. We hadn't thought of reading the map like that.

"That makes so much sense!" Moe said with a burst of excitement.

"Yuki, you could be right," Fatima said excitedly. "The coastlines may change, but not the mountains and cliffs. Look at these mountains on the bottom left of the map. Now, look to our right. See those mountains? These have to be the same mountains."

"If that is true, then the left of the map has to be the north," I said.

"This is very interesting! Look at these two small stars near the moon." Moe said eagerly.

"Yes, as we know, that is to show it's night," said Yuki.

"But could it mean something more? Could these stars be Dubhe and Merak, usually called the pointer stars of the Big Dipper? Look at this large star after the arrow. Maybe this is Polaris, the North Star, showing this is the northern hemisphere!" Moe's eyes were sparkling.

"There is one way to check!" Aisha exclaimed. "Measure the distance between the pointer stars. The North Star should be roughly four to five times this distance."

We measured the distance using a twig, and not surprisingly the distance between the small stars and the big star was about five times the distance between the smaller stars!

"Wow! These people knew so much about stars and cardinal directions!" Fatima said excitedly.

"But what do these other symbols and markings around the edges mean?" Liam asked.

"These, at the bottom, towards the right of the moon, look like letters, but they aren't making sense."

"And what are these numbers on top?" Moe asked.

"Usually, pirates would hide messages using ciphers and cryptic clues," said Yuki.

"And look at these drawings. This one is an octopus and this is a fish." Carlos said.

"And this is the sword the pirate used to kill the fish!" laughed Liam.

"And this could be an hourglass!" Aisha said.

"Pirates during those times depicted dangers using sea creatures, many of them were mythical. This could be a warning of some kind. But I don't know what." Yuki said.

Moe added, "These drawings here on the left show a bunch of trees. Then again, some creature…"

"This is all so complicated! These could be random images used to fill up the space. Maybe we are overthinking! I agree with what Yuki said about the directions. Captain Salazar has indeed intelligently hidden the clues to the real directions. But the rest could be images, letters, and numbers, only to confuse the reader of the map. Isn't that a possibility?" Liam asked.

Nobody had an answer.

"I say, we follow the map and reach these mountains where the X mark is shown," Liam said.

"Guys, this is so exciting! How many people get a chance to go on an actual treasure-hunting expedition?" Fatima tried to change the mood. It worked.

We decided to sleep early that day after packing our bags and leave as soon as there was light the next morning.

That night was longer than the previous night. We were getting ready to go on a treasure hunt. We had only seen it in movies or read in books. Till this day, most of us thought that pirate treasures were only stories. But here we were set to follow the directions in a map we found in a cave.

We lay listening to the sound of the waves washing up on the shore. At that moment, it seemed that we were no longer straining our ears to listen to the sound of a ship or a rescue helicopter.

We needed some more time on this island.

CHAPTER 11

We gathered essentials – knife, rope, flashlights, magnifying glass and bottles filled with stream water.

We set out on our little expedition. Yuki stayed back and assured us she would be safe.

We trekked for a couple of hours, sometimes losing our way in the dense growth of trees. We took short breaks in between to sip water and catch our breath. But our excitement was such that we did not feel tired.

After a short trek, we reached the stream. We knew we had to cross it and then trek to the right towards the mountain range. We had fished in the shallow waters near the bank. But there was no way to determine the depth in the middle. The stream now looked much wider, now that we had to cross it.

"If we face upstream and walk carefully, where the water reaches below our knees, we can cross it safely. We only need to look for a stable crossing point with a firm bottom. The depth cannot be more than 3-5 feet." Liam said.

"But we don't know that for sure. There are some places where the water is slowing down. This could mean that it is deeper there. We don't even know how deep. I don't think it is a good idea to cross the stream on foot." Fatima said.

"It's not only the depth. There could be pebbles and rocks at the bottom. If we lose our balance, we could end up getting our stuff wet. Worse, the map could get wet. We can't risk that." Moe said.

"Let's go left and walk towards the source of the water. It cannot be far. Then we go around these mountains and reach the other side of the stream. All we have to do then is to follow the stream on our right and we will reach these mountains." I said.

The trek wasn't as short as we thought.

We trekked for more than two hours before we saw huge mountains from where the water was rushing out.

We walked around the mountains, finding our way through dense vegetation, to reach the other side of the mountains and then the stream. Several hours had passed. The sun was now shining bright.

We rested briefly and set out again.

After a few hours, we reached a fork where the stream split to the left. We followed the stream and finally saw the mountains ahead of us! We did not realize the size of the mountains from the map. In front of us were huge mountains, the peaks of each visible from where we stood. They looked majestic.

We slowly and steadily made our way to the third mountain, as the X mark was made specifically on it.

After about half an hour of uphill trek, we stumbled upon a towering cliffside. "Look!" shouted Carlos, "There is something on this rock here." His voice was brimming with excitement.

There was a huge rock with carvings on it!

We looked at the carvings, marveling at the sight. The carvings depicted scenes of sea battles, mythical creatures, a small ship, a boat and a large ship.

Was this ship the Savage Gale?

We ran our fingers slowly over the carvings, feeling the indentations on our fingertips.

One carving showed a person walking away from the sea, towards us. This had to be Captain Salazar himself, with his signature flat nose and a fierce expression, clutching what looked like a box or a chest. We kept staring at the pirate. It was like he was standing right in front of us looking into our eyes. We were looking at a piece of history, that no one else in the world knew about!

There was a huge rock with carvings on it!

These look like footprints.

"We are likely the first ones to be seeing and touching these carvings in over 500 years!", said Carlos.

"Yeah! But where is the treasure? I only see rocks here! Where do we dig? He couldn't have made us trek for half a day to witness his piece de resistance!" Liam said impatiently.

We searched all around but couldn't find anything of value. We looked at each other expecting someone to come up with an answer.

Finally, Aisha broke the silence, "The more I look at it, I feel this is not just a work of art. There is no reason for Salazar to come all the way here and carve line art on rock. This is some kind of a message. These have to be clues. I'm sure following these clues will lead us to the actual treasure. Captain Salazar is trying to defend his treasure. Look how he is holding the box close to his chest. He can't be giving it away so easily."

We looked at the carvings carefully, trying to find hidden clues. The carvings showed a large ship, sinking, and a person fighting with what looked like a sea serpent. People lay dead, floating on the water. There were giant spider or octopus-like creatures with tentacles. One of them had two of its tentacles cut off. There was another smaller ship with a man brandishing what could be a sword. Maybe, he was the one who cut the tentacles.

Captain Salazar was walking towards us, clutching his chest.

"Flat Nose seems to have fought with these mythical sea creatures and then killed everyone on board who tried to take his treasure. They could be Blackthorn's crew!" I said excitedly.

"Yes! That little spot could be blood dripping from his sword hanging by his side." Fatima pointed to the sword. "Yuki would have been so excited." She said.

"And look at these impressions towards the right. These look like footprints. These are leading to these trees, so these might be directions." Moe said.

"There is a similar drawing in the map we found earlier," Aisha said. "Look here, this could be drawn to depict an island with palm trees or coconut trees."

"Yes! And then there are markings going towards these mountains. This is exactly like the map. So we are at the right place," said Moe.

"So, we are saying these carvings only establish that we are at the right place. But there are no real directions to find the treasure!" Liam spoke frustratedly.

Disappointed and disillusioned, we sat on the rocky surface, figuring out our next steps.

"Look! What's this?" We heard Aisha, her voice full of wonder.

Aisha was sitting down on her knees a few feet away, looking intently at another huge rock.

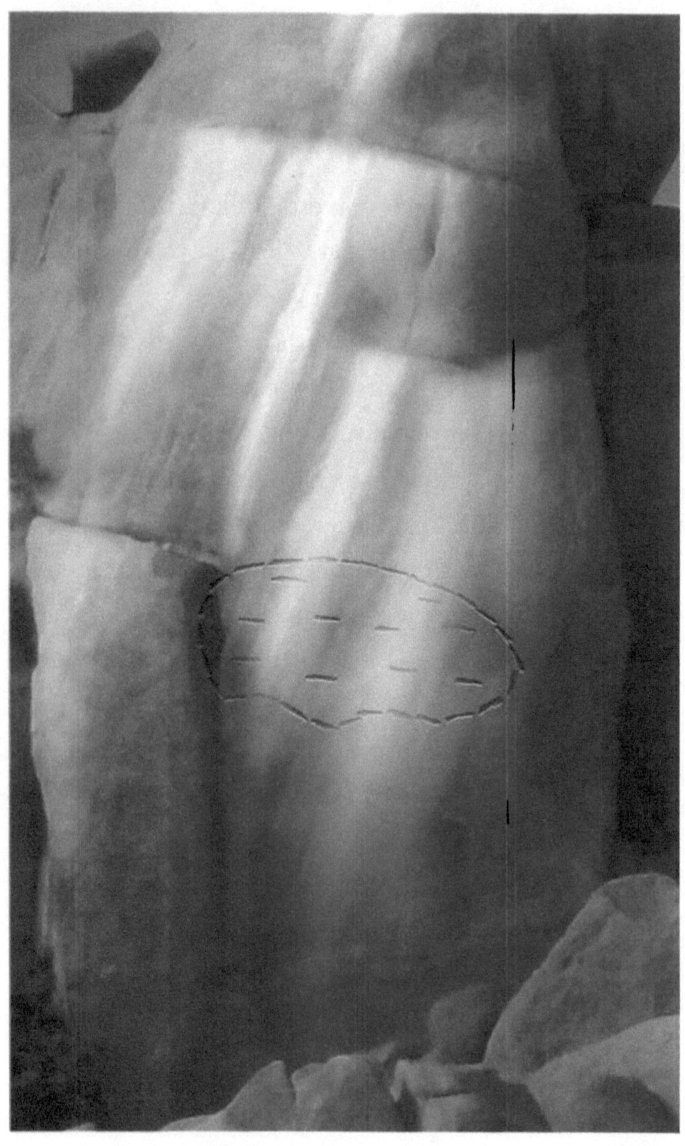

"It looks like an unfinished carving!"

There was a large oval-shaped carving. But it looked incomplete and didn't make any sense. There was a stream of white residue left by rainwater running from the top of the rock. The rain water had discolored the surface of the rock, running over the carving, almost destroying it.

"It looks like an unfinished carving!" Moe said.

"Why would he carve something like this and leave it unfinished? I'm sure it means something." I said thoughtfully.

"Maybe he had originally carved something but this watermark has destroyed the original carving," said Fatima.

"It's called efflorescence," said Aisha. "When rainwater moves through the rock, it dissolves salts. The salts are left behind as crystals when the water evaporates, forming this pattern. The composition of this rock seems different from others. That's why you find the water stain on this rock and not on others."

"Ok, Einstein! Maybe this is where the treasure is," I said teasingly.

We looked around to see anything that might look like an oval patch of land. There was none we could spot from where we stood.

"Since this carving is made much below the level of the main carving, it could be a clue telling us to go down from here," Fatima said.

"Here is a way to go down from here," Moe said.

We all looked at where Moe was pointing. It was a deep drop through trees and boulders. The vegetation was so thick that we couldn't see how deep the drop was. Not only did the path look treacherous, but we did not know what was down there. Maybe it's a bottomless pit.

"We have come so far, let's do it," said Carlos. He was the first to go down holding onto shrubs, vines, and trees, carefully keeping each step. We followed. We were sitting on the ground, practically lying on our backs, slowly sliding down. One missed step and we will go tumbling down.

Occasionally small rocks rolled downwards when we stepped on the ground.

"Aaaaah!"

That was Fatima! She lost her foothold and slid fast. She went crashing down.

Chapter 12

Moe was quick to hold her arm, while himself holding onto the root of a tree. While Fatima stopped in her tracks, several boulders from under her feet went tumbling down, crashing through the vegetation, the sound getting feeble over time. It took a few seconds for the sound of the rocks to stop and we realized that we are several feet above the ground and a fall from here would mean death.

Once Fatima took a moment to catch her breath, Moe shouted, "We should go back!"

"No, let's do this," Fatima said. "We have come so far. Let's finish what we started."

We agreed to continue.

We kept each step carefully and after a very long time, we saw a ridge along the side of the cliff, going around it to our left. We reached the ridge. It was a narrow path, about two feet in width, the big cliff on one side, where we were descending from, and a 30-foot drop on the other.

We gasped in horror. If Moe hadn't held Fatima's arm, she could have ended down there!

We reached the narrow ridge.

"How exactly do we go back?" Liam asked. None of us knew. But, now, there was no turning back.

"If Captain Salazar found a way to carry the treasure here and go back to carve it on the cliff, we will too," Moe said, lightening the mood. He had made a point.

Holding onto the cliff on the left, we walked through the narrow pathway, trying not to lose our footing. After a few minutes, we heard what sounded like a dull rumbling. We were walking towards the sound. The sound increased as we moved ahead. After some time, we saw a huge waterfall from a distance and there was a large oval-shaped natural plunge pool. From a distance, the shape of the pool looked exactly as it was carved on the cliff. As we walked closer to the waterfall, we could feel the refreshing spray of water on us. The path was also now slippery, with the spray of the water, so we had to keep each step carefully.

We realized the genius mind of Captain Salazar. The rainwater staining on the cliff, or efflorescence as Aisha put it, depicted the waterfall.

We reached the waterfall, kept our bags on the ledge and jumped into the pool. It was the most refreshing swim we ever had. All our tiredness vanished.

It was picturesque from up here. But we didn't have a camera to capture these moments. We didn't care.

"So, where's the treasure? Liam asked, jolting us back to reality.

We looked at each other and then around us. There was no place to go from here. The water from the pool fell 30 feet below and there was nowhere to go from here but back.

"We are missing something. The treasure has to be here." Carlos said and took a deep dive inside the pool. Moe and Fatima joined.

I looked for areas around the pool where the treasure could be hidden.

They soon came up above the water. "It's difficult to see anything underneath because of the fall, and it doesn't look like a place where Captain Salazar would keep a treasure chest," said Moe. "Even if he did, we can't find in this water," added Carlos.

"Did we miss any other clue on the cliff?" asked Fatima. "Should we go back and check?" She asked.

We were losing heart. We will now have to go back the same way we came, and there was no easy way to go up the cliff. We remembered the boulders tumbling down.

"It will be easier while going up. We will be holding onto trees and vines for support," Moe assured.

Now that we had a plan, we felt more assured. "Let's relax for now and we will leave in some time," said Fatima. We will never get to experience this ever. Aisha and Carlos swam to the waterfall. They stood under the fall soaking in the experience, splashing water. We spent several minutes playing in the pool.

"It's time to go," Carlos shouted after a while and swam back. "If we leave now, we can get back to the beach before dark."

Liam was already up on the ledge, drying himself with his tee. He helped Fatima up. Carlos was sitting on the ledge admiring the scenic beauty from that height. If it wasn't for us being marooned on this island, tour organizers would charge a fortune for this view.

"Where's Aisha?" Moe asked. She was nowhere to be seen. We suddenly felt a sense of panic. Did she drown? Maybe she went too close to the verge.

Without another thought, Liam and Carlos jumped back into the pool. They dived under while Fatima and I swam to the verge. She was nowhere!

CHAPTER 13

"Moe! Liam! Guys!" we heard a faint, stifling, cry. It was Aisha. But she was nowhere in sight. Maybe she fell over the verge and was holding onto her life.

Just then Aisha emerged from inside the waterfall! Her eyes were gleaming. "You won't believe this! Come with me," she said and swam back straight into the waterfall and disappeared.

Not knowing what this was, we followed. A large gush of water fell on us. We made our way into the fall, following Aisha.

Behind the curtain of the fall was a cataract cave! It was large, the size of a 10 feet by 10 feet room. We looked around us, bewildered.

"There's more," Aisha yelled. "Look at this," she pointed to one end of the cave. We followed her. There was a small hole on the other side. No! It was a secret tunnel!

"I will get our stuff," said Carlos excitedly, and went back. We were tingling with excitement and curiosity. We might have found the treasure!

"This tunnel is very narrow. I don't know what's waiting inside." Said Moe, apprehensively.

"I could feel the wind through this tunnel," said Liam, sitting on his knees bent over, shining his flashlight inside the tunnel. "There has to be an opening on the other side. I would take my chances instead of going back to climbing the cliff."

The entry to the tunnel was narrow. There was only room for one to crawl through the passage.

"If we get stuck in between, we won't be able to turn around. We can't even turn our heads," said Moe.

He was right. The tunnel was dark and if we were to get stuck between the rocks, there was no way out. But right now, this seemed worth taking a chance.

Liam took the lead. Slowly, he crawled into the tunnel and moved ahead. Fatima was next keeping a safe distance. Carlos was third. I was next, followed by Aisha. Moe was the last to enter. We moved without speaking. We could only hear each other breathing. We could feel the lack of oxygen in that confined space. What could have been a few minutes seemed like hours. We didn't know if this was the right decision, but we had come so far, there was no turning back.

My knees were paining, crawling on the hard rocks. I think I scraped my elbow too. The wind was getting stronger. After about fifteen minutes of crawling through the tunnel, I heard Liam's voice. It wasn't clear. But it sounded happy. I heard Fatima's voice next. "Another minute," I told myself. After a few more grueling minutes, I saw light over Carlos' shoulder.

Finally, I was out.

I tumbled out to the floor of what was a small cave. I lay there along with others for a moment before we all started laughing with relief. Till a moment back we were unsure whether we would get out of that tunnel. We all had bruised our knees. But we were finally out.

The entrance to the cave was covered with dense vegetation. Carlos inspected and said, "The path from here looks straight. Let's find a way to get back before it gets dark."

"Doesn't that … look like an arrow?" asked Moe, still lying on the floor looking up at the roof.

We followed his gaze, and there was a small arrow carved on the roof. That was it. No other carvings.

"It has to mean something," Moe said.

"There is a crevice there!" Fatima said, stretching her neck. The crevice was almost invisible.

"I will climb and check," Liam said.

Liam did free climbing as a hobby and wouldn't pass an opportunity to hang by the cliffs.

He took a moment to look around for places to hold and then ran his palms on the walls of the cave.

Then like an expert gymnast, he jumped and clung to a jagged projection of the rock wall, his feet searching for footholds. He moved from one point to the other, swiftly leaving his previous hold, fingers gripping tightly around the rough, weathered edges.

Finally, he was near the crevice. He looked at it and while still hanging from one rock, he put his hand inside the crevice and pulled out something.

We all looked at this show with amazement. Liam climbed down with the object, jumping down the last few feet.

It was another parchment again rolled up neatly!

Chapter 14

The parchment was stained in a deep, golden-brown color, with edges that were curled and frayed. A thin, stiff, leather cord was wrapped tightly around it.

We gathered around, barely breathing, our eyes wide with excitement. We all were quiet. Our hearts were pounding with awe and curiosity. Could this really be the map leading to the treasure?

With trembling hands, Liam slowly untied the brittle cord. Dust floated in the air as Liam unrolled the parchment. It was a message written in a stunning, flowing script. The letters were perfectly aligned with each other. It was difficult to believe that someone could write with such finesse.

Moe quickly brushed the dust off the floor with his hands, as Liam gently placed the parchment down.

We were reading a message written by Captain Salazar himself. This was historic already.

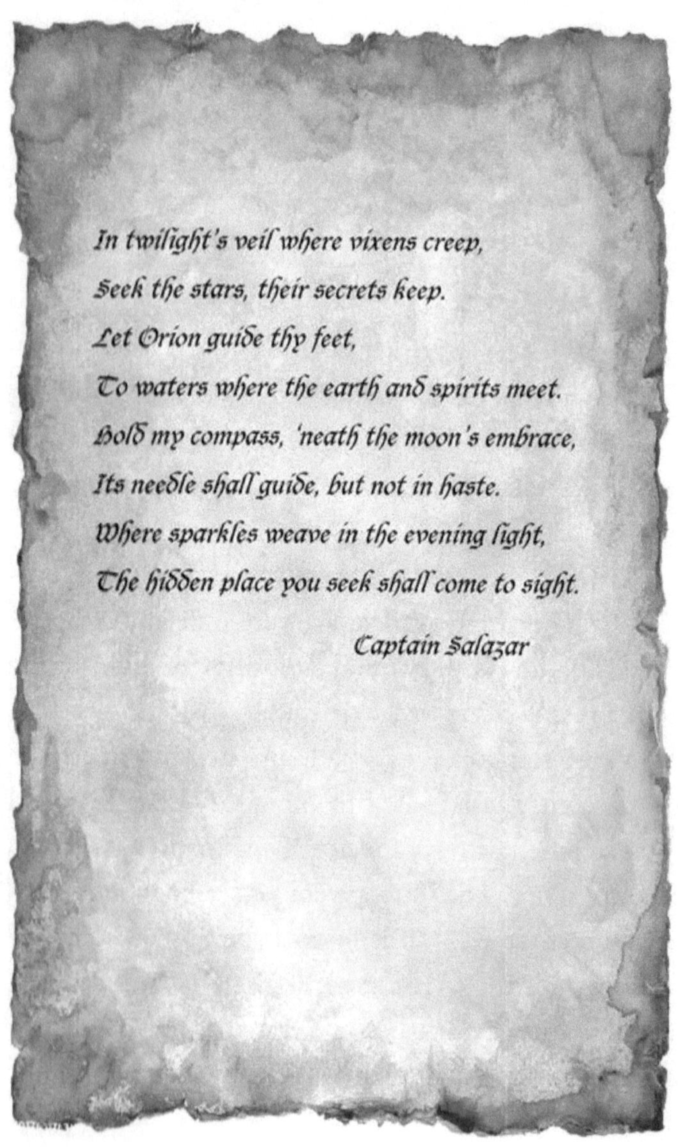
In twilight's veil where vixens creep,
Seek the stars, their secrets keep.
Let Orion guide thy feet,
To waters where the earth and spirits meet.
Hold my compass, 'neath the moon's embrace,
Its needle shall guide, but not in haste.
Where sparkles weave in the evening light,
The hidden place you seek shall come to sight.

Captain Salazar

"Huh? What does this mean?" asked Fatima. "Why can't he write in simple words?"

"The reason for him leaving a string of clues is to ensure that the treasure doesn't fall into the wrong hands. Only those who have the grit and intelligence to solve the riddles have the right to the treasure." Aisha said. "Let's go through the riddle. I'm sure we can solve it."

We all agreed.

"*Twilight's veil.* This should refer to sunset, when the moon is out." Said Fatima.

"Right. But more specifically, twilight is the time between day and night when the sun is just below the horizon. That's a duration of only about 30-45 minutes, at best." Moe explained.

"A vixen is a female fox. That's all I understand from this," said Fatima. "So, the time during sunset when the foxes are out."

"*Seek the stars, their secrets keep.* This sounds like using celestial navigation. Maybe, hinting at constellations." Said, Carlos.

"Yes! They depended on the stars for navigation during those times. Look he is talking about Orion guiding us. Orion's belt is composed of three prominent stars – Alnitak, Mintaka, and Alnilam – the brightest of the three," said Moe.

"But what about *earth and spirits* meeting?" I asked.

"I have heard that in ancient times, people believed that the spirit of their ancestors floated on the sea waters. So, we are looking for a location, which is somewhere along the sea." Liam said.

"It can't be," Aisha said. "It says, this is a *hidden place* and there is water. So, it's a hidden water body on land, not the sea. In those times, the earth would have meant land. So, this place is somewhere inside the island. A water body, hidden from plain sight."

"You are right. We will need to use our compass once we reach there and it will show us the treasure!" Fatima said excitedly.

"It says here *Hold my compass*, not just any compass. I have a feeling that we will get to know more once we reach there." I said confidently.

"We should move now," Moe said looking at the sky. "The message stresses on 'twilight'. We have to find the hidden water body before it gets dark." He spoke with a sense of urgency.

The excitement was palpable.

"Yuki is alone." Carlos reminded us.

It was true that in the excitement we had forgotten about Yuki. We all were quiet.

Fatima broke the silence. "We are this close to finding the treasure. We don't even know the way back. We should carry on and find the hidden water place before it gets dark. Yuki can take care of herself. We wouldn't be here if it wasn't for her. She would want us to find the treasure. Nothing would make her happier. We owe this to her."

"Let's move!" Moe said again.

We came out of the cave and pushed our way through the thick vegetation. The sun was about to set. We didn't have much time. We had to find the water body and find the treasure during twilight.

Moe continued, "The sun is about to set. In twilight, we have to follow the Orion belt to reach the hidden water place and find Captain's compass to locate the treasure."

"True. We will have to move fast. Once it gets dark, we won't be able to solve this." Carlos supported.

The sun set in a few minutes. We kept looking at the sky for the stars to shine. And they did.

"There! That's the Orion belt!" cried Moe.

There were three stars in one straight line.

Carlos shone his flashlight and started walking in the line of the stars. We followed looking at the sky to make sure we were headed in the right direction.

It was a challenge to find our way in the darkness. While we had an idea about the direction to take, looking at the stars and walking was not the same as walking the city streets with street signs. To top it, we had limited time to reach our destination. We couldn't afford to get it wrong. The jungle is an unforgiving place to be lost.

"Aaah!" Liam fell, tripping over the root of a large tree. His flashlight went flying and hit a rock. It went off. The glass was shattered.

We heaved Liam up. Nothing major. Just a bruised elbow. His shirt was torn and the flashlight was unusable.

We were losing time.

"One of us should follow the Orion belt. The rest should focus on our path ahead. Otherwise, this trip could be dangerous and we will never reach the water body", said Fatima.

We all agreed.

Moe was assigned the job of following the sky and we focused on the path in front. Carlos took up the job of making sure that Moe did not fall. He kept giving directions.

We realized that walking in a straight line wasn't possible in the jungle with thick undergrowth and big trees everywhere. We kept weaving in and out of trees and walked for what seemed like hours.

We strained our ears for any waterfall. None.

After about 20 minutes of leaving the cave, we saw a sparkling glow ahead of us.

Chapter 15

"There!" said Liam, pointing in the direction of the glow. We all quickened our pace and reached there.

It was a magnificent sight. There was a beautiful lagoon tucked away inside the jungle. It was formed such that one could not spot it from the sea or land till you reached near it. There were huge trees and mountains on either side.

Just like the message said, the lagoon was right in line with the Orion belt. The water had a magical, glowing hue. The water with its gentle waves looked like it's sprinkled with stars!

It was an unbelievable sight. We went to have a closer look.

Indeed, the water was glowing. It was a mix of blue and green light. Like little stars in the water. An almost otherworldly sight, as if the water was alive and pulsating with light.

Aisha went closer to the water and inspected it. "It's bioluminescent algae, also called dinoflagellates.

The glow happens due to a chemical reaction. When these algae get disturbed—like when waves crash or fish swim through them—they release light. It's kind of like a natural glow stick! In ancient times, people would have thought this is magic!" She explained, her eyes wide with excitement.

"It's amazing! It's no less than magic!" Fatima said.

"Ok, so we have found the water place, where *sparkles weave in the evening light.* Now, where is Captain Salazar's compass? It will be dark soon!" Carlos said.

We all looked around for anything that looked like a compass.

Liam saw that on one wall of a mountain, a rock seemed to be unnaturally fixed. It didn't look like a natural fit. He intuitively pulled at the rock. It moved but did not come off.

Carlos joined Liam in moving the rock. After a few moments of pulling and pushing, the rock fell off. There was a large hole that looked man-made. Inside was an ornate rectangular brass box. There was a little latch on the box.

While the latch did not give away initially, after a few minutes of trying, the latch opened. Inside the box was a beautifully made compass with a brass casing and a brass key. The box was otherwise empty.

The compass was circular, with a thick crystal top. The dial was marked with cardinal directions N, E, S, and W and divided into degrees. The markings were engraved into the dial. Outside the crystal, there were several markings around the compass.

We stood admiring the exquisite craftsmanship.

Liam took out the compass and read the directions.

"The compass seems broken. It's showing erratic directions. It keeps spinning. Maybe because it has been sitting here for 400, 500 years." Liam said. He hit the compass a few times to see if the spinning stops. It didn't.

"Liam, bring it over here to the water!" Moe called out. "We have very little time left!" The sense of urgency was clear in his voice. "The message says,

Hold my compass, 'neath the moon's embrace,

Its needle shall guide, but not in haste.'"

"Hold it slow and steady where the glow is the brightest," Aisha said.

Liam held the compass in the middle where the sparkling was the most prominent.

Suddenly as if by magic, the needle moved in its axis and stopped steady, pointing to true North.

We looked at this magic in amazement!

CHAPTER 16

"He is making us go around in circles!" Liam said. "You didn't expect him to send you a message with the 'live map location' of the treasure. Did you?" Quipped Fatima.

"Recalculating route. Turn left from the big tree in 200 steps. Continue straight for 100 steps. Take the exit on the right. Your destination is 100 feet down. Go jump!" Aisha said in a deadpan tone.

We laughed.

"I understand the need for showing the path using constellations but why did we have to use the compass in the glowing algae water? Compass works the way it's supposed to work, water or not!", wondered Fatima.

"Yes! And why *'twilight'*? We could have used the compass in the daytime or even after sunset. Why did it have to be that hour?" Carlos asked.

"They would have thought everything unexplainable to the human mind was some kind of magic or the work of spirits!" Fatima said.

"Maybe. But I can't get over the fact that the compass was spinning erratically when I got it out of the hole in that rock. The moment it touched the water, it was still and showed us the direction. How do you explain that?" Liam sounded flustered.

"Is there a mystical connection between the light of the setting sun and the bioluminescent algae in the lagoon?" Carlos wondered.

"I have read that the twilight is the time when the veil between the physical world and the spiritual realm is thinnest. Could there be spirits of dead pirates guarding the treasure?" Liam sounded scared.

Moe didn't say anything. He kept shining his flashlight on the compass, maybe admiring the detailed work. After a while, he got up and walked towards the rocks.

Sitting here, by these waters, was the most blissful experience I have ever had.

What we saw today was nothing short of magic.

"I think I know why". Moe said waving his arms, calling us to the rocks. "Look how the compass starts spinning when it comes closer to the rocks. There is something about the composition of these rocks, that makes it rich in iron, hematite, or some other magnetic minerals. This is the reason for this anomaly. The compass will not show the actual direction near the rocks. Captain Salazar knew this very well.", he said.

We were excited about this discovery. I looked at the rocks closely. "Yes, look at this rusty color. There are mineral veins and textures on these rocks!" I said, running my fingers over them.

"It all makes sense now!" Carlos jumped in. "Once the compass is held over the bioluminescent algae in the water, the surrounding environment is somehow neutralizing the magnetic interference. The water is acting as a buffer, reducing the influence of the rocks, allowing the compass needle to stabilize and point true north!" He spoke eagerly. His eyes were wide with excitement and surprise.

"That's not only it. Look how the compass looks under the light." Moe said while shining the flashlight on the compass. The cardinal directions were engraved at all points around the dial. There was East, West, North, and South in all directions!

"Under normal lighting, we can never make out the actual direction. But now look under the water. Only E and 20 degrees are lit up! These are the real directions.", Moe said.

He was right. We had missed this.

"This means we have to head towards 20 degrees East!" said Moe.

"This is brilliant! I have read that in earlier times, navigators coated their compasses with natural bioluminescent material, such as Chitin, a natural polymer found in the shells of crustaceans, like shrimp and crabs, or extracts of certain species of phytoplankton. They mix it with natural binders such as beeswax or plant resin. This coating remains inert in daylight but reacts to the chemical environment of the algae, causing it to glow!". Aisha said.

We were amazed at the brilliant mind of Captain Salazar. Not only did he ensure that the treasure could only be found by those who had the determination, intellect, and a strong heart, but he also possessed very advanced knowledge of science. We were beginning to respect Captain Salazar. Our preconceived notions of the pirates as crude, illiterate, and savage were shattered. What we witnessed today was a stark contrast to the image we had long held of them.

"But where is the treasure?" asked Carlos. "We have a key but we don't know what it opens." He spoke with frustration.

"Maybe there's no treasure. This was his field test to recruit new pirates." Said Liam, chuckling.

Fatima took the box in her hands and turned it around several times, inspecting it closely. Under the lid was a brass metal plate with several jumbled-up letters. She slowly removed the metal plate from the box. It had something written on it.

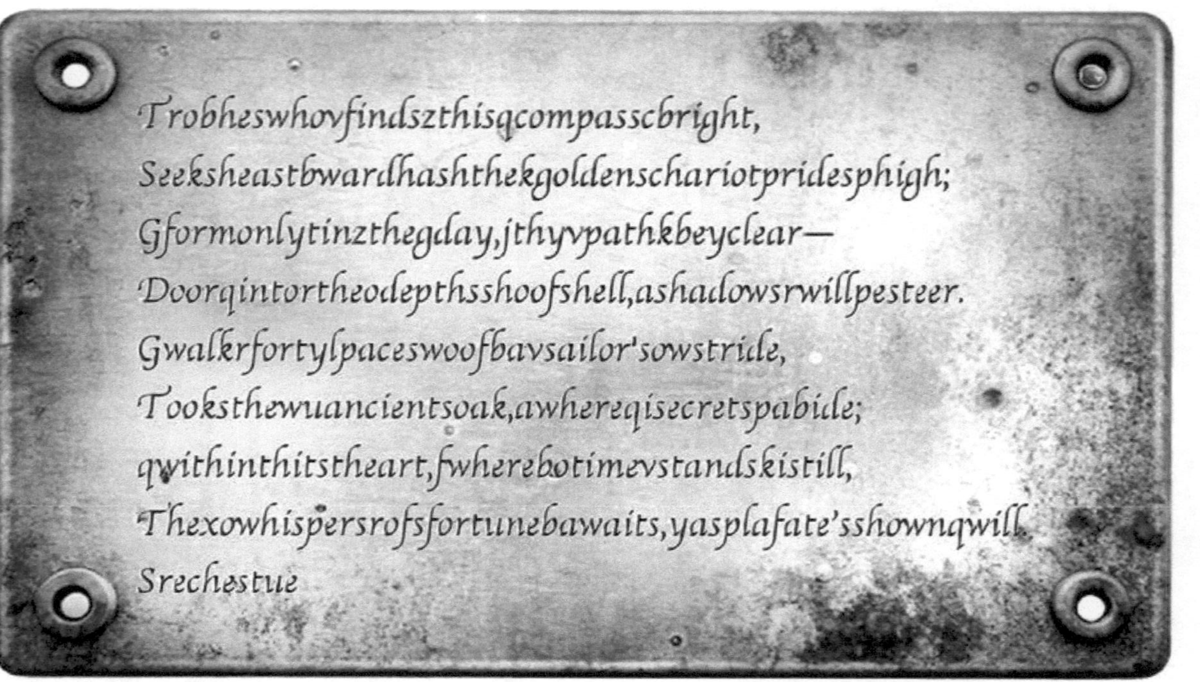

Trobheswhovfindszthisqcompasscbright,
Seeksheastbwardhashthekgoldenschariotpridesphigh;
Gformonlytinzthegday,jthyvpathkbeyclear—
Doorqintortheodepthsshoofshell,ashadowsrwillpesteer.
Gwalkrfortylpaceswoofbavsailor'sowstride,
Tooksthewuancientsoak,awhereqisecretspabide;
qwithinthitstheart,fwherebotimevstandskistill,
Thexowhispersrofsfortunebawaits,yasplafate'sshownqwill.
Srechestue

"These look like letters. But they don't make any sense." She sighed.

We crowded around her to look at the letterings.

"Why don't we see it under the water?" Moe asked. "I'm sure these waters play an important role for Salazar to refer to it in his message."

We took the metal plate to the water body and carefully lowered it into the bioluminescent water, and for a moment, nothing happened. Then, slowly parts of the inscription began to glow.

Moe was right! Slowly, only those letters that Captain Salazar wanted us to read started glowing!

Chapter 17

Letters flickered to life, not all at once, but in scattered patches. Soft ripples of water reflected and danced on the metal plate. The cold water shimmered, tiny glowing specks drifting around the plate.

Slowly, only some words revealed themselves in front of our wide, astonished eyes. If we hadn't witnessed this spectacle, we wouldn't have believed it!

Nobody spoke. We just stared, caught between wonder and disbelief. It felt like magic.

The message now started to make sense.

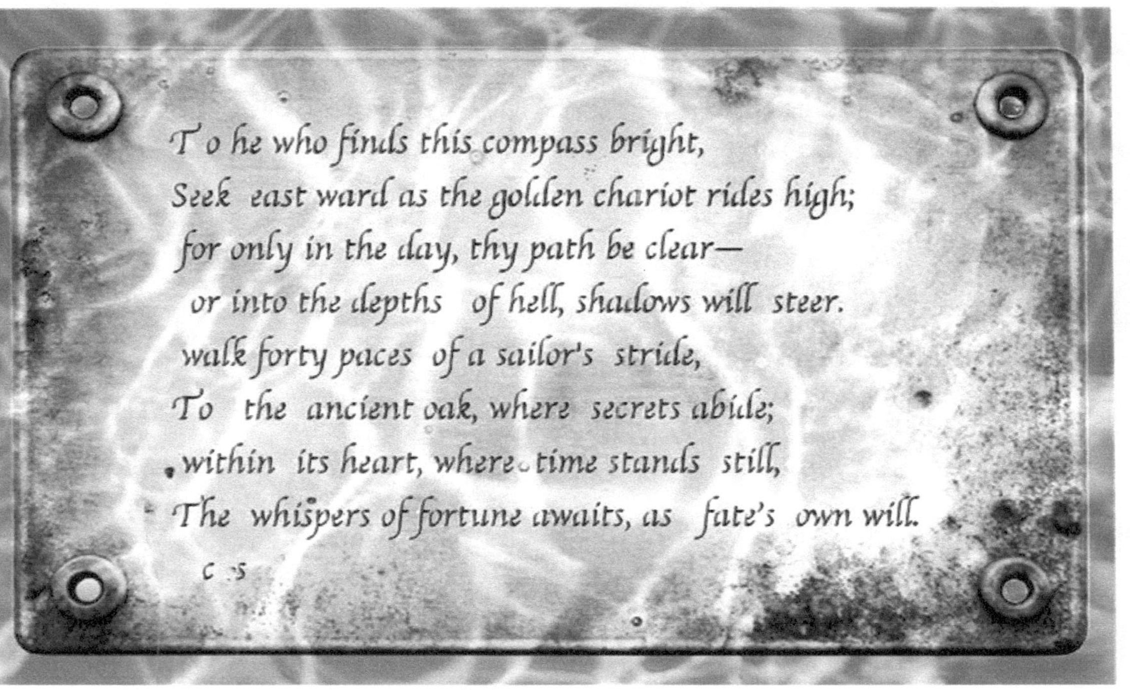
To he who finds this compass bright,
Seek east ward as the golden chariot rides high;
for only in the day, thy path be clear—
or into the depths of hell, shadows will steer.
walk forty paces of a sailor's stride,
To the ancient oak, where secrets abide;
within its heart, where time stands still,
The whispers of fortune awaits, as fate's own will.
c s

Finally! We were close to the treasure!

"The Captain is asking us to go east. We know through the compass, the direction to take." Liam stated the obvious.

"But what's a golden chariot? Is that the treasure? A chariot made of gold?" Carlos asked.

"No. No. The golden chariot is the sun. In many ancient books, the sun was depicted as a God who travelled on a golden chariot." Said Aisha excitedly.

"But he is asking us to go only during the day," said Fatima.

Carlos was getting impatient. With the treasure somewhere nearby, it was difficult to hold us back. He said, "Why wait till day? We have flashlights. Maybe pirates of those times did not have solar batteries. I say we go eastward right now." He asserted.

"It's not only about going east; he is warning us about the depths of hell if we don't heed his advice. Do you want to take a chance going against the advice given by a man of this intellect?" Fatima asked.

"Maybe there's nothing to it, mate. But I suggest we wait till daybreak. We are tired anyway. Let's start fresh in the morning." Moe said, putting his arm over Liam's shoulders.

"Ok. Let's solve the rest," said Liam excitedly. "What's forty paces of a sailor's stride?"

"A sailor's stride could be a bit longer than average due to the way sailors often navigate on a ship, where they need to take longer strides," Carlos said.

"Are we then looking at walking 40 steps?" asked Fatima.

"No! One stride is two steps. So, we are looking at 80 steps," said Moe.

"Interesting! One step for an average 5 feet 10 inches man is usually about 15 inches. So, one stride is 30 inches or 2.5 feet. So, we are looking at walking 100 feet!" Aisha did some quick mental math.

"The average height of people would have been lower in the 16th century. But, let's go with these numbers." Carlos said.

"So, we need to walk about 100 feet towards 20 degrees east, where we will find an ancient oak tree. Wonderful!" exclaimed Liam.

"Let's get some rest now. We will start early." Moe said.

It was dark now. In the excitement of this hunt, we had missed eating throughout the day. We were famished and tired but that didn't seem to bother us right now.

As we lay on the ground, trying to sleep, Fatima asked, "What do we do with the treasure?"

"We divide it into seven," Liam said, almost immediately.

"Shouldn't we inform the authorities?" asked Aisha.

"Why do they need to know? Finders keepers." Liam said.

"And how exactly will you carry it with you? The authorities will know." I said.

"I think we should inform the authorities. They could excavate the place. Find more treasure. We will become famous and rich!" Moe said.

"I will keep some part of the treasure before we inform the authorities." Said Fatima.

"If we are ever found, Fatima," said Carlos. "Otherwise, we will live on this island with all that treasure and nowhere to go."

Reality set in. We were losing count of days.

Chapter 18

We woke up early the next day. Today, was the day of truth.

We walked towards the east, 20 degrees as shown in Captain Salazar's compass. Our pace was quicker today, in anticipation of the treasure. Moe was leading us.

"Mates, here is your Captain Flat Nose!" Carlos tried doing a sailor's stride. He walked with a confident tilt, shoulders back, and head held high, with long strides. He didn't see himself stepping on a round pebble and slipped. He landed on the ground with a loud thud.

Thwack! The branch of a tree broke and landed right on his nose.

"Oof!" Reacted Carlos, cupping his nose with his palms.

"Yeah, right!" said Liam, trying to stifle a chuckle, "now you are indeed Flat Nose!"

For a moment there was silence. Then everyone started laughing, the sound echoing through the forest.

Carlos got up with a sheepish smile, dusted himself off, and said with his chin up:

"Dear mates, remember that a sailor may stumble and land in the dirt,

But true courage is in rising again, brushing off his hurt!"

We all clapped. This was beginning to be a fun adventure.

We kept walking through the woods.

"Stop!!!" we heard Moe yelling. He had his arms spread out wide, gesturing for us to stop in our tracks. He was looking down.

We slowly walked up to Moe. It was a horrifying sight. We were standing on the edge of a large pit about 8 feet wide and 10 feet long. It was so deep inside that we couldn't see its bottom!

"Now I see why the captain said, '*Or into the depths of hell, shadows will steer.*' This is the depths of hell he spoke about. If we had ventured out in the night, we would have never seen this pit. Since it is at the edge of the path, with a deep drop, we wouldn't have seen it even with our flashlights!" I said worriedly.

Our hearts beating fast, we walked around the pit, walking along the edge but keeping a safe distance. We reached the other side of the pit. "How do we measure the distance now?" asked Moe.

"We covered about 60 feet till the pit. The pit is about 8 feet wide. So, let's take it around 68 to 70 feet. Another 30 to go", Carlos said.

We continued walking, but now even more cautious about any other dangers. Our strides became shorter than usual.

After about ten feet, emerging from behind several other large trees, we saw a huge oak tree, just like Captain Salazar said!

"Magnificent!" said Aisha.

There it stood, in all its grandeur. Its vast, old trunk twisted upward. The thick, weathered bark was deep brown and gray. The deep fissures told the story of Captain Salazar's exploits. Its roots stretched out like the fingers of giants, anchoring the tree firmly in the earth.

Chapter 19

The canopy of leaves spread wide, rustling softly in the breeze, casting shadows on the ground below. When sunlight filtered through the leaves, it created a magical mosaic of light and shadow on the floor.

"Let's look for the treasure!" shouted Carlos, breaking the spell. "The scroll says,

'Within its heart, where time stands still,

The whispers of fortune awaits, as fate's own will.'

What is the heart of the oak tree?" he asked.

Aisha and Moe were already going around the tree, looking for either an opening or a way to climb up.

"Look over here!" That was Aisha. We ran to where she stood. She was removing several pieces of wooden planks, stacked against the tree. The planks were weathered and worn, their surfaces cracked and splintered. As she picked them up, they crumbled easily in her hands, breaking apart with a brittle snap. As the planks were removed, it revealed a wide opening in the trunk of the oak tree.

Aisha turned to look at us. Then after taking a deep breath, she exhaled slowly. We will now know if all this was just a joke or if we were steps away from finding a 16th-century treasure.

She slowly made her way into the trunk of the tree through the opening.

We followed her inside to find a hidden chamber. Its walls were thick with sturdy bark. There was a strong smell of wood in the air. Sunlight filtered in through small openings, illuminating the walls.

The floor was covered in soft moss, like a natural carpet. Right in the center, sat a large box half buried in the moss.

Crafted from sturdy, dark wood, the chest was adorned with intricate carvings of mythical sea creatures and swirling waves. Its surface was polished but worn, with several scratches and dents. The box had handles dangling from either side. Moss had grown on the chest. But it still looked sturdy and strong.

We stared at the chest with astonishment.

The chest was secured with heavy iron chains, rusted but still strong. A large, ornate lock, shaped like a scorpion, held the lid in place.

Liam shook Moe's shoulder. He was staring at the treasure chest as if under a spell. Moe quickly unzipped the side pocket of his cargo and fished out the key we found at the lagoon. He handed it to Liam.

Liam inserted the key in the lock and turned it clockwise. There was no movement.

It was stuck. Then anti-clockwise. There was a brief moment of resistance.

'Clunk!' There was a loud, heavy, sound and the lock sprung open.

Liam slowly creaked open the heavy lid.

What we saw, was much more magical than we anticipated.

There was a dazzling array of gold coins, gleaming even in this dark hollow space, their surfaces marked with the insignia of ancient kings. Beside them, there were strings of pearls and shimmering gemstones, reflecting the little sunlight that had found its way inside the trunk. They reflected hues of deep blue, green, and fiery red.

Among the treasure were some other relics of the sea: a weathered compass, a dagger, jewelry; and a few small, curious trinkets.

Carlos dug his hands into the chest and pulled out a handful of coins, slowly and dramatically letting them fall back into the chest. Fatima giggled. She joined in, inspecting the various trinkets.

I picked up a ring and wore it. It fits perfectly. It had a lion's head carved on it.

We all took turns digging our hands into the treasure chest. This was better than the movies.

"How do we carry it?" asked Liam, trying to lift the heavy chest. It refused to budge.

"Is that another map?" asked Aisha, pointing to another parchment scroll, which revealed itself when Carlos removed the coins. It was about the same size as the map we found in the cave.

Was it the directions to another treasure? Or, the way to get out of this island?

Chapter 20

Aisha carefully reached into the treasure chest and pulled out the parchment scroll. It was dry and fragile. The edges were curled. A fine layer of dust scattered into the air as she lifted it.

Her fingers were steady, but she held the scroll delicately. This parchment was thicker, heavier, with a leathery texture. There were faint creases on its surface.

We leaned in, our eyes locked onto the scroll.

Aisha hesitated only for a moment before slowly unrolling the parchment. As it unfurled, we realized it wasn't just one page—it was two, carefully rolled together. The pages were covered in flowing, intricate script, the ink still legible. The letters swirled in elegant loops and sharp strokes.

This wasn't just any message. It was the voice of Captain Salazar himself.

Aisha held her breath, her eyes scanning the text. Then, with a steady voice, she began to read.

Aisha unfurled the entire parchment. It read:

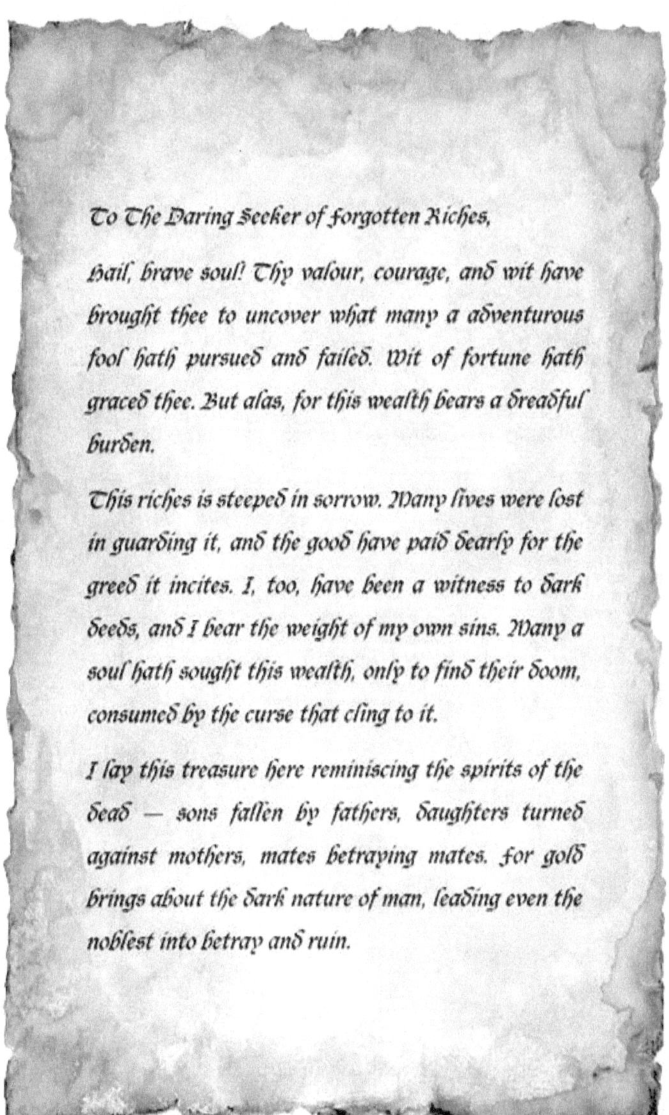

As thou standest before the treasure, ponder well thy merit to claim such. Shouldst thou decide to keep these hidden riches, ask thyself: Will it serve the greater good? Shall each gold piece bring forth joy and peace, or shall it evoke greed and treachery?

If thou art to donate this burden upon thy king, thy emperor, or thy kin, ponder whether they shall use it with glory. Will they use it for noble deeds, or will it bring forth further bloodshed?

If doubt lingers in thy heart, then leave it be, as thou found it. Let it rest in silence, untainted by sinful desire. Speak not of it to the birds nor the spirits that dwell herein, for silence may be thy shield against the fury of the slain.

May Poseidon, Lord of the Deep, grant thee wisdom and fortune to find thy true destiny.

In Shadows,

Captain Salazar

We looked at each other. There were words and phrases we didn't fully understand. But we understood what Captain Salazar wanted to say.

He was warning us of the treasure's dark history as it was 'blood money', responsible for the loss of many innocent lives. He was warning us that greed can awaken our dark side, and even the closest of us could betray each other. He was asking us to reflect on our own worthiness to take the treasure and to think well about whoever else we hand it over to.

We sat on the moss-covered floor. There was this chest of treasure in front of us, waiting to be taken. Yet, even after centuries, Captain Salazar wielded power over this treasure. His mere words were enough to get us thinking.

"Would we ever betray each other over money?" Fatima broke the silence.

We wanted to say No. But we didn't. We couldn't. Maybe the power of the wraiths guarding the treasure didn't let us speak.

"Let us leave," Carlos said.

"And the treasure?" Moe asked.

"Let's not take it, Moe," I said.

"Yeah. You are right. This is too scary. I already feel a heavy burden on my soul. I would rather get back home and sleep peacefully on my bed. I can't live with the weight of owning gold, which was made by killing people." Fatima said.

"Let's then inform the authorities about this place once we get back," Moe said.

"I think not," Liam said thoughtfully. "Look at the power Captain Salazar has over us. The onus of the treasure falling into the right hands is on us, the finders of this treasure. If any wealth from this is not used for the goodness of people, the responsibility is on us." He sounded anxious.

"You are right, Liam." Aisha agreed. "And then all the agencies, from archaeology, border protection, treasury, to law enforcement and several others will come here and destroy this beautiful heaven. When they set up camp to study the ecosystem, they will end up destroying the lagoon as well. They will dig up the island, cut down trees, and destroy this place. Let's not tell anyone about this." She said earnestly.

"Yes, this will be our secret," Liam said. He bent down and locked the treasure chest.

We took one long look at the treasure, which we had been longing to have, but are now leaving on our free will.

"I feel a sense of freedom. I feel light" said Carlos, as we stepped out breathing fresh air.

Chapter 21

We set out on our trek back to the beach. We had to walk westward, which, we were sure. We had a few bananas on the way back. We had hardly eaten anything since yesterday.

We kept making marks on trees to ensure we did not go around in circles. We trekked for several hours, during which we passed by many cliffs, streams, and small and large caves. While we wanted to explore the caves, we knew better than to disturb the silence of any treasure, which might be hidden by Captain Salazar. We felt his presence around us, watching us, guiding us.

We finally reached a cliff on the west end of the island. We could look around from here.

"There!" cried Fatima. We spotted Yuki standing on the waters about 200 feet away looking into the sea. We waved and called out. She couldn't hear us.

We trekked down the cliff and quickly walked to our spot on the beach. Strangely, it felt like getting back home.

Yuki saw us from a distance and burst out crying. Fatima ran and hugged her. We all joined.

"I thought I had lost you all. Maybe you were killed by wild animals or you lost your way!" Yuki was smiling and crying.

"You thought you could shake us off, didn't you? Surprise! We are back, and we are not going anywhere!" Moe said.

"How is your foot, Yuki?" asked Liam.

"Much better. Look, I can walk now." Said Yuki, limping around.

"I have something to tell you. I saw a ship. It was very far, and I don't know whether it was a cargo ship or a passenger ship. It looked like a matchbox from here. I don't even think they saw me, but I flashed a mirror at them and also waved. They didn't stop." Yuki said sadly.

This was our first hope, however small. Maybe Captain Salazar was indeed guiding us.

"What did you guys do? Did you find the treasure?" Chuckled Yuki. "Maybe you are getting it delivered by freight." Yuki laughed.

Though it took a moment for us to gather our thoughts, Carlos immediately quipped, "Yeah, we found the treasure."

We all looked at Carlos with surprise.

He continued. "Since we couldn't carry it, we went to the nearest bank and deposited all the gold and silver.

We will withdraw as cash once we get back home. I'm buying a Ferrari."

We all laughed.

"It was a dud, Yuki. We searched around but didn't find anything. Even if there were treasure, it has been found and taken by other pirates or treasure hunters," said Liam.

CHAPTER 22

The next day in the wee hours, we were shaken awake by a loud whirring sound. We jumped up from our bed of leaves, to see three choppers circling our beach!

Is this true? A rescue team? We ran to the shore waving our hands, some of us tripping and falling on the golden sand.

"Help! Help!" We cried.

The choppers circled a few times, dropped some packets to the beach and then took off immediately.

We looked at the image of the choppers becoming smaller and smaller in the clear blue sky. We couldn't believe what just happened. Did they leave us behind?

Carlos crashed on his knees in the waters, crying, looking towards the location of the choppers. "Why? Why?"

Moe ran up to us. "They have dropped food packets, guys!" he said. "These were scout helicopters. Seems they couldn't land on this beach. Don't worry, man! We are getting rescued for sure!" He hugged Carlos.

Reassured, we ran back to where they had dropped the food packets. Fatima and Aisha had already ripped apart the packets. It had a large quantity of ready-to-eat meals, energy bars, nuts, and canned fruits. vegetables, soups, and several cases of bottled water.

We ripped open the packets and ate whatever we could. After several days, the count of which we had started to forget, of eating bananas and berries, this was a godsend. Once our stomachs were full, we lay down on the beach.

Moe was lying beside me. He said in a hushed tone, "Now I believe it. Captain Salazar is watching over us."

Though it defied logic, I couldn't disagree. How else could this miracle happen?

In a few hours, we saw the choppers again, circling above us.

And then we saw a boat in the distance. It was fast. It reached us in a few minutes and stopped very close to the shore. It was a Boston Whaler 320 Outrage.

Immediately a few crew members jumped into the water and a uniformed man stepped down using a small ladder. He waded through the waters and approached us. He had a wide, warm smile.

"Are you the passengers who were on board Mistral?" he asked, looking at the lifeboat. The lifeboat we had secured was rocking rhythmically, bobbing up and down, water lapping its sides with the waves created by the rescue boat.

Fatima ran and hugged him, crying, "Yes! Yes! Yes! Thank you. Thank you!"

He smiled, held Fatima by her shoulders, and said, "Let's go back home."

✳ ✳ ✳

Chapter 23

The captain went back to the boat and had a conversation with the crew. He then disappeared for a very long time and then came out, animatedly talking to the crew.

Meanwhile, the medics did a quick check. Vital signs, temperature, hydration, injuries, fatigue, mental state, infections, allergies, insect bites, rashes. A stretcher was called for Yuki.

Once we were inside the boat, the captain briefed us. "Once we get back to the mainland, you will be taken for a medical assessment and then taken to a safe shelter. There could be some interviews with rescue teams, law enforcement, and other agencies to understand what happened in Mistral. There could be a psychological evaluation, but you all seem fine. It's standard procedure. You will be quarantined for some time if we find any infectious diseases. Your families have already been informed, and they will be waiting for you. ETA is tomorrow 0700 hours"

He led us to a cabin that could house all of us. It was compact, with a small bathroom, sink, and sleeping space for four. There was a refrigerator and storage compartment.

"You will find clean clothes in the storage. Take rest. You have a long day tomorrow. You will find the refrigerator well-stocked. If you need anything else, let me know." He spoke.

"What about other passengers?" I asked.

"You are the only survivors," said the captain and closed the cabin door.

Our mood was suddenly heavy with shock and disbelief. We struggled to process this new information.

After a long time, we showered in warm water and slept on comfortable mattresses. There was enough food, clean sheets, and a feeling of safety.

We didn't get up with sand on our clothes, body, and hair. We didn't feel cold. There were separate bottles of water. We wore clean clothes. We brushed our teeth. We didn't have to look out for snakes and scorpions.

We went to sleep reminiscing and reflecting on the last few days.

We woke up early the next morning and met outside on the deck. The cool breeze was refreshing. There were some sandwiches and canned juice waiting for us. We had our breakfast and stood by the deck railing, waiting to touch land.

We all took our spots and stood staring into the deep sea, which looked calm and serene.

Moe stood at one corner. He looked at the sea, which had devoured hundreds of lives but acted as if everything was normal.

Aisha smiled at herself looking into the sea. She knew she was safe.

Fatima and Yuki sat together on a bench. We will be home soon. Our parents would be waiting for us.

Liam and Carlos stood looking around knowing that there would be other islands, with more stories, and treasures.

I wanted to reach back home. Sleep in my bed. Turn off my alarm and sleep till late, snuggled up in my cozy blanket.

ABOUT THE AUTHOR

Ishan, the imaginative mind behind this book, has been crafting stories since he was 7 years old. Inspired by the incredible books he's read, Ishan loves creating new worlds where he can explore, control the action, and invite readers to join the adventure. At just 10 years old, he has a gift for combining action, humor, and brain-bending puzzles that challenge readers to think on their feet.

When Ishan isn't writing, he's usually designing and building using construction blocks, racing scale model cars, or finding creative ways to master sandbox games. He also enjoys whimsical adventures and challenges in his favorite video games.

He believes stories aren't just about reading—they're about feeling like you're part of the action. That's why his stories are filled with interactive twists and puzzles that put YOU in the driver's seat.

Ishan's debut novel is the ultimate mix of thrills and brainpower. Whether you're solving mysteries, dodging danger, or unlocking secrets, this adventure is designed to keep you hooked.